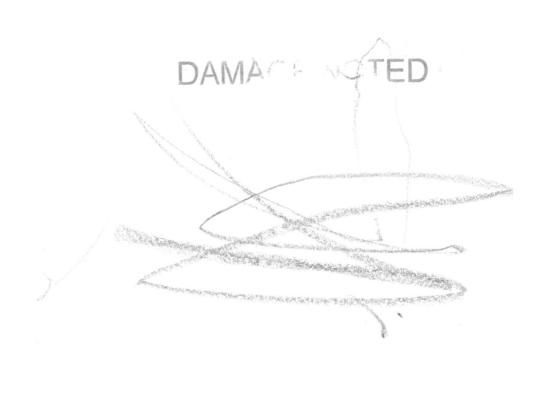

Christmas Tree!

For David and Stephen

—W.M.

For Judy Stevens and her Christmas spirit

—F.M.

Christmas Tree!
Copyright © 2005 by Wendell and Florence Minor
Manufactured in China.
All rights reserved. No part of this book may be used or reproduced in any
manner whatsoever without written permission except in the case of brief
quotations embodied in critical articles and reviews. For information address
HarperCollins Children's Books, a division of HarperCollins Publishers,
1350 Avenue of the Americas, New York, NY 10019.
www.harperchildrens.com

Library of Congress Cataloging-in-Publication Data
Minor, Wendell.
    Christmas tree! / Wendell and Florence Minor.— 1st ed.
       p.   cm.
    Summary: Christmas trees come in all shapes and sizes and can be found
in almost any setting, but there is only one "best" Christmas tree.
    Includes bibliographical references.
    ISBN 0-06-056034-7 — ISBN 0-06-056035-5 (lib. bdg.)
    [1. Christmas trees—Fiction. 2. Christmas—Fiction. 3. Stories in rhyme.]
I. Minor, Florence Friedmann. II. Title.
PZ8.3.M6467Ch 2005   2004022753
[E]—dc22   CIP
                                                                 AC

Typography by Wendell Minor and Al Cetta
1 2 3 4 5 6 7 8 9 10   ❖   First Edition

Christmas Tree!

WENDELL AND FLORENCE MINOR

KATHERINE TEGEN BOOKS

An Imprint of HarperCollinsPublishers

Christmas
is
here!
Imagine
that you are
a Christmas tree.
What kind of tree do
you think you could be?

A tree so high it would touch the sky?

Or a tree
so small it would
fit in the wall?

A tree
that would sing
when Christmas
bells ring?

Or a tree
so bright
it would light
up the night?

$\mathbf{A}$ tree that
was made for a
city parade?

Or a tree
that's at home where
the buffalo roam?

**A** tree
that could
float on
top of a
boat?

A tree
just
for dogs,

Or one
that's for
cats,

O r one
just for
horses—
how
about that?

A tree where
there's snow,

Or
there's
lots
of sunshine . . .

N_{o!}
The
best tree
of all is the
one that is mine!

MERRY CHRISTMAS

The
oldest
known record
of a Christmas
tree is from 1551, in
Strasbourg,
Germany.
Decorations on early
Christmas trees consisted
of mostly candy,
fruit, and nuts.
Candles were used to light up
Christmas trees beginning in 1708.
The first known Christmas tree in America
was in Bethlehem, Pennsylvania, in 1746.
The first record of a Christmas tree in a large
American city is from Philadelphia, in 1825.
Christmas trees were first displayed in Boston in 1832,
Texas in 1846,
and San Francisco in 1862.
In the 1890s, tradition held that Santa Claus brought
children a Christmas tree along with their toys on Christmas Eve.
Only one in five American homes had a Christmas tree in 1900.
By 1930, Christmas trees could be seen all across America.
Electric lights first appeared on a Christmas tree in America in 1901, and they have been
keeping Christmas bright ever since.

SOURCE

Snyder, Phillip V., *The Christmas Tree Book: The History of the Christmas Tree and Antique Christmas Tree Ornaments* (New York: The Viking Press, 1976).